This Little Hippo
book belongs to

With love to Liz and Rob,
for being super.
P.K.

Scholastic Children's Books,
Commonwealth House, 1-19 New Oxford Street,
London WC1A 1NU, UK
a division of Scholastic Ltd

London • New York • Toronto • Sydney • Auckland

First published in the UK in 1998 by Little Hippo,
an imprint of Scholastic Ltd

Copyright © Peter Kavanagh, 1998

ISBN 0 590 19687 1

My Dad, the
SUPERHERO!

Peter Kavanagh

Little Hippo

Is it a bird? Is it a plane?
No, it's my Dad, the Superhero.

Today we were going to do lots of playing. My Dad is great at playing games.

When he has time.

Poor old Dad. He's always
flying off to deal with trouble.

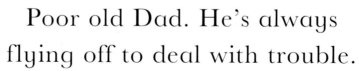

Everyone in the whole
world needs my Dad.

He's great at saving people from terrible disasters. And when it comes to fighting monsters there is nobody as good as my Dad.

My Dad, the Superhero, has so
much important work to do . . .

. . . that he hardly ever has time to hang around and just play – like I do.

Sometimes he
wishes he could
play a game
with me.

But then he gets
an urgent call and
WHOOSH,
he's off again.

So I go and see what Mum is doing.

She doesn't know what time
Dad will be home.

Mum says it's not easy being a
Superhero and Dad will play with
me when he gets a chance.

But I don't know when that will be.
Waiting makes me sad.

One day I had this great idea.
I took my binoculars and climbed
out on to the roof.

From up there I could see for miles.
Maybe I could watch Dad at work.

But my foot slipped and suddenly
I knew I was in big trouble.
"DAAAAAD!"

Far away, around the world,
somehow, Dad heard me.

He dropped what he was doing
and flew faster than any Superhero
had ever flown before!

He saved me just in the nick of time.

I explained about the binoculars,
my great idea and all the waiting.

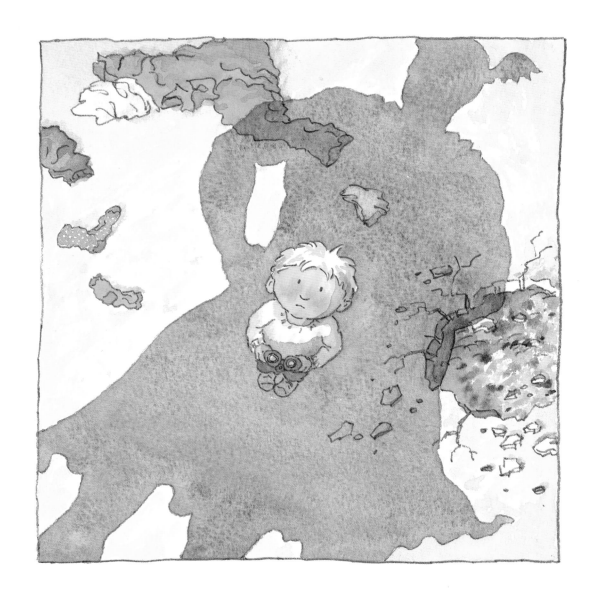

I thought I was really in big trouble
this time.

But Dad just gave me a Super-hug
and said we had better sort things out.

Is it a bird?
Is it a plane?

No, it's me and my Dad
playing a great game.